For Lovers of
FOOD
& DRINK

EDWARD LEAR

Compiled by
Vivien Noakes &
Charles Lewsen

COLLINS
ST JAMES'S PLACE, LONDON
1978

William Collins Sons and Co Ltd
London · Glasgow · Sydney · Auckland
Toronto · Johannesburg

First published in 1978
© Vivien Noakes and Charles Lewsen 1978
ISBN 0 00 222235 3
Set in 10 on 12 point Ehrhardt
Made and Printed litho in Great Britain
by W & J Mackay Ltd, Chatham

Plumbunnia Nutritiosa

Introduction

There is a tradition in the Lear family that Edward's father was sent to jail for debt, and that his mother went daily to the prison taking with her "a full six-course dinner with the delicacies of the season". Certainly Lear believed that giving and sharing food was a gesture of affection. In the Pelican Chorus, Princess Dell marries the King of the Cranes, who "won that heart, With a Crocodile's egg and a large fish-tart". After years of travel in countries whose strange food perhaps inspired his nonsense recipes, Lear settled in Sanremo, bribing his friends to visit him with promises of nonsense menus. His actual meals he noted in his diary: ". . . rather shady soup, tongue up=be=warmed, & beans done in a new – but let us hope – a seldom way". "Very 'sublime' dinner—(now restricted to one dish)—of roast veal & my own broad beans." "It is funny to see what attention I always pay to 'dinner' details," he wrote, "but I have a notion that food is a great factor in our fooly life." This was particularly true for Lear, for he suffered from epilepsy and knew that unwise eating might bring on an attack. Neverthe-less, he looked forward to the next "eggzistens" with "a few well behaved small cherubs to cook & keep the place clean", when he would "sit for placid hours under a lotos tree a eating of ice creams & pelican pie".

CRUEL

. . . t'other day I dined at Ld. Fitzwilliam's, where we complained of the chairs bitterly, as being hard & quite round – or as Ld. F said – like ostrich eggs. You kept spinning round, & by no means could balance yourself with dignity, expecting constantly to fall quite off.

1.

O Digby my dear
It is perfectly clear
   That my mind will be horridly vext,
If you happen to write,
By ill luck to invite
   Me to dinner on Saturday next.

2.

For this I should sigh at
That Mrs. T. Wyatt
   Already has booked me, o dear!
So I could not send answer
To you – "I'm your man, Sir! –
– Your loving fat friend,
      Edward Lear."

I asked the girl here – (having a friend to dine, & wishing to have the wine cool,) for some Ice. But she thought I said, "I want some *mice*," – & was seized with great fear forthwith.

. . . if you come here directly I can give you 3 figs, & 2 bunches of grapes: but if later, I can only offer you 4 small potatoes, some olives, 5 Tomatás, & a lot of Castor oil berries. These, if mashed up with some crickets who have spongetaneously come to life in my cellar, may make a novel, if not nice or nutritious Jam or Jelly.

Here is the paradigmatical illustration of last Sunday's dinner.

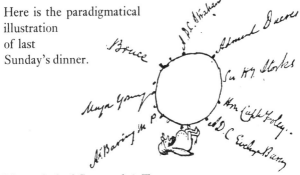

Dinner, 'ashed Carves ed, & Toemartyrs.

There was an Old Person of Dean,
Who dined on one Pea and one Bean;
For he said, "More than that would make me too
    fat,"
That cautious Old Person of Dean.

Mrs. Jaypher found a wafer
which she stuck upon a note;
This she took and gave the cook.
Then she went and bought a boat
Which she paddled down the stream
Shouting, "Ice produces cream,
Beer when churned produces butter!
Henceforth all the words I utter
Distant ages thus shall note –
'From the Jaypher Wisdom-Boat.'"

Plum-pudding Flea,
Plum-pudding Flea,
Wherever you be,
O come to our tree,
And listen, O listen, O listen to me!

O criky! – here's a go! as the Flea said when he jumped into the middle of the plate of apricots and found nothing to eat.

The Biscuit Tree
This remarkable vegetable production has never yet been described or delineated. As it never grows near rivers, nor near the sea, nor near mountains or vallies, or houses, – its native place is wholly uncertain. When the flowers fall off, and the tree breaks out in biscuits, the effect is by no means disagreeable, especially to the hungry. – If the Biscuits grow in pairs, they do not grow single, and if they ever fall off, they cannot be said to remain on. –

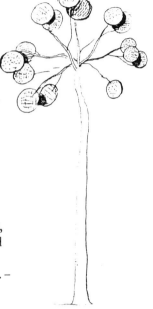

G was a Gooseberry,
Perfectly Red;
To be made into Jam
And eaten with Bread.
g!
Gooseberry Red!

The Two Old Bachelors

Two old Bachelors were living in one house;
One caught a Muffin, the other caught a Mouse.
Said he who caught the Muffin to him who caught the Mouse, –
"This happens just in time! For we've nothing in the house,
"Save a tiny slice of lemon and a teaspoonful of honey,
"And what to do for dinner – since we haven't any money?
"And what can we expect if we haven't any dinner,
"But to lose our teeth and eyelashes and keep on growing
                                                    thinner?"

Said he who caught the Mouse to him who caught the Muffin, –
"We might cook this little Mouse, if we only had some Stuffin'!
"If we had but Sage and Onion we could do extremely well,
"But how to get that Stuffin' it is difficult to tell" –

Those two old Bachelors ran quickly to the town
And asked for Sage and Onion as they wandered up and down;
They borrowed two large Onions, but no Sage was to be found
In the Shops, or in the Market, or in all the Gardens round.

But some one said, – "A hill there is, a little to the north,
"And to its purpledicular top a narrow way leads forth; –
"And there among the rugged rocks abides an ancient Sage, –
"An earnest Man, who reads all day a most perplexing page.
"Climb up, and seize him by the toes! – all studious as he sits, –
"And pull him down, – and chop him into endless little bits!
"Then mix him with your Onion, (cut up likewise into Scraps,) –
"When your Stuffin' will be ready – and very good: perhaps."

Those two old Bachelors without loss of time
The nearly purpledicular crags at once began to climb;
And at the top, among the rocks, all seated in a nook,
They saw that Sage, a reading of a most enormous book.

"You earnest Sage!" aloud they cried, "your book you've
                                    read enough in! –
"We wish to chop you into bits to mix you into Stuffin'!" –

But that old Sage looked calmly up, and with his awful book,
At those two Bachelors' bald heads a certain aim he took; –
And over crag and precipice they rolled promiscuous down, –
At once they rolled, and never stopped in lane or field or town, –
And when they reached their house, they found (besides
                                    their want of Stuffin',)
The Mouse had fled; – and, previously, had eaten up the Muffin.

They left their home in silence by the once convivial door.
And from that hour those Bachelors were never heard of more.

There was an Old Person of Hurst,
Who drank when he was not athirst;
When they said, 'You'll grow fatter,' he answered,
                              'What matter?'
That globular Person of Hurst.

The Excellent Double-
extra XX imbibing King
Xerxes, who lived a long
while ago.

Bassia Palealensis

What is the difference between a member of parliament, & a beer barrel with nothing in it?
One is M.P. the other M.T.

P. was some punch
Made ready for lunch,
But which nobody tasted
And so it was wasted.
    P!
All that good Punch!

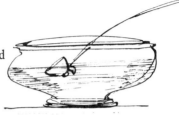

There was an Old Man of Dumbree,
Who taught little Owls to drink Tea;
For he said, "To eat mice is not proper or nice,"
That amiable Man of Dumbree.

Two Receipts for Domestic Cookery

To Make An Amblongus Pie

Take 4 pounds (say 4½ pounds) of fresh Amblogusses, and put them in a small pipkin.

Cover them with water and boil them for 8 hours incessantly, after which add 2 pints of new milk, and proceed to boil for 4 hours more.

When you have ascertained that the Amblongusses are quite soft, take them out and place them in a wide pan, taking care to shake them well previously.

Grate some nutmeg over the surface, and cover them carefully with powdered gingerbread, curry-powder, and a sufficient quantity of cayenne pepper.

Remove the pan into the next room, and place it on the floor. Bring it back again, and let it simmer for three-quarters of an hour. Shake the pan violently till all the Amblongusses have become of a pale purple colour.

Then, having prepared the paste, insert the whole carefully, adding at the same time a small pigeon, 2 slices of beef, 4 cauliflowers, and any number of oysters.

Watch patiently till the crust begins to rise, and add a pinch of salt from time to time.

Serve up in a clean dish, and throw the whole out of the window as fast as possible.

Knutmigrata Simplice

Bottlephorkia Spoonifolia

To Make Gosky Patties

Take a Pig, three or four years of age, and tie him by the off hind leg to a post. Place 5 pounds of currants, 3 of sugar, 2 pecks of peas, 18 roast chestnuts, a candle, and 6 bushels of turnips, within his reach; if he eats these, constantly provide him with more.

Then procure some cream, some slices of Cheshire cheese, four quires of foolscap paper, and a packet of black pins. Work the whole into a paste, and spread it out to dry on a sheet of clean brown waterproof linen.

When the paste is perfectly dry, but not before, proceed to beat the Pig violently, with the handle of a large broom. If he squeals, beat him again.

Visit the paste and beat the Pig alternately for some days, and ascertain if at the end of that period the whole is about to turn into Gosky Patties.

If it does not then, it never will; and in that case the Pig may be let loose, and the whole process may be considered as finished.

Time will show as the Lobster said when they
assured him he would become red if he fell into the
boiler.

O was an Oyster
Who lived in his Shell,
If you let him alone
He felt perfectly well.
o!
Open-mouth'd Oyster!

The Dolomphious Duck,
who caught Spotted Frogs for her dinner
with a Runcible Spoon.

I am in a very unsettled condition, as the oyster
said when they poured melted butter all over his back.

The New Vestments

There lived an old man in the Kingdom of Tess,
Who invented a purely original dress;
And when it was perfectly made and complete,
He opened the door, and walked into the street.

By way of a hat, he'd a loaf of Brown Bread,
In the middle of which he inserted his head; —
His Shirt was made up of no end of dead Mice,
The warmth of whose skins was quite fluffy and nice; —
His Drawers were of Rabbit-skins; — so were his Shoes; —
His Stocking were skins, — but it is not know whose: —
His Waistcoat and Trowsers were made of Pork Chops; —
His Buttons were Jujubes, and Chocolate Drops; —
His Coat was all Pancakes with Jam for a border,
And a girdle of Biscuits to keep it in order;
And he wore over all, as a screen from bad weather,
A Cloak of green Cabbage-leaves stitched all together.
He had walked a short way, when he heard a great noise,
Of all sorts of Beasticles, Birdlings, and Boys; —
And from every long street and dark lane in the town
Beasts, Birdles, and Boys in a tumult rushed down.

Two Cows and a Calf ate his Cabbage-leaf Cloak; —
Four Apes seized his Girdle, which vanished like smoke; —
Three Kids ate up half of his Pancaky Coat, —
And the tails were devoured by an ancient He Goat; —
An army of Dogs in a twinkling tore *up* his
Pork Waistcoat and Trowsers to give to their Puppies, —
And while they were growling, and mumbling the Chops,
Ten Boys prigged the Jujubes and Chocolate Drops. —
He tried to run back to his house, but in vain,
For Scores of fat Pigs came again and again; —
They rushed out of stables and hovels and doors, —
They tore off his stockings, his shoes, and his drawers; —
And now from the housetops with screechings descend,
Striped, spotted, white, black, and gray Cats without end,
They jumped on his shoulders and knocked off his hat, —
When Crows, Ducks, and Hens made a mincemeat of
that; —

They speedily flew at his sleeves in a trice,
And utterly tore up his Shirt of dead Mice; —
They swallowed the last of his Shirt with a squall, —
Whereon he ran home with no clothes on at all.

And he said to himself as he bolted the door,
I will not wear a similar dress any more,
Any more, any more, any more, never more!

There was a Young Lady of Greenwich,
Whose garments were border'd with Spinach;
But a large spotty Calf, bit her Shawl quite in half,
Which alarmed that Young Lady of Greenwich.

"Do you go much into Society?" said the Snail to the Oyster.
"Certainly knot" – replied the Oyster.

Did you ever eat a monkey stewed in Treacle? I'm told it is a crack Ceylon dish.

There was an Old Man of the East,
Who gave all his children a feast;
But they all ate so much, and their conduct was such,
That it killed that Old Man of the East.

. . . so completely did silkworms seem the life and air, end and material, of all Staíti, that we felt more than half sure, on contemplating three or four suspicious-looking dishes, that those interesting lepidoptera formed a great part of the groundwork of our banquet – silkworms plain boiled, stewed chrysalis, and moth tarts.

We halted at the khan of Episkopí, close to a little stream full of capital watercresses which I began to gather and eat with some bread and cheese, an act which provoked the Epirote bystanders of the village to ecstatic laughter and curiosity. Every portion I put into my mouth, delighted them as a most charming exhibition of foreign whim, and the more juvenile spectators instantly commenced bringing me all sorts of funny objects, with an earnest request that the Frank would amuse them by feeding thereupon forthwith. One brought a thistle, a second a collection of sticks and wood, a third some grass; a fourth presented me with a fat grasshopper – the whole scene was acted amid shouts of laughter, in which I joined as loudly as any. We parted amazingly good friends, and the wits of Episkopí will long remember the Frank who fed on weeds out of the water.

There was an Old Man of Vienna,
Who lived upon tincture of senna;
When that did not agree he took camomile tea,
That nasty Old Man of Vienna.

There was an Old Man of El Hums,
Who lived upon nothing but Crumbs,
Which he picked off the ground, with the other birds round,
In the roads and the lanes of El Hums.

The Hasty Higgledipiggledy Hen,
who went to Market in a Blue Bonnet and Shawl,
and bought a Fish for her Supper.

The Nutritious Newt,
who purchased a Round Plum-pudding
for his Grand-daughter.

Mrs. Jaypher
    said "It's safer,
If you've Lemons in your head;
First to eat,
    a pound of meat,
And then to go at once to bed.
Eating meat is half the battle,
Till you hear the Lemons rattle!
If you don't, you'll always moan;
In a Lemoncolly tone;
For there's nothing half so dread=
    =ful, as Lemons in your head!"

What will happen to me, as the oyster said when he
very inadvertently swallowed the Gooseberry bush,
nobody can tell.

I have left off wine totally – by Dr. Hassall's order, – but en ravanche, I drink surprising quantities of beer – & shall bye and bye become like this. . .

Hassall irritates me with his d – – d Thermometers & Barometers. As if I couldn't tell when an Eastwind eats me in half – spite of the thermometer – by reason of sunshine, – being ever so high!! I told him just now that I had ordered a Baked Barometer for dinner, & 2 Thermometers stewed in treacle for supper.

. . . may the toes of those who lyingly profess to love winter, never be warm! May they cease to know the difference between their toes and their fingers and may both be turned into icicles and afterwards mixed up in ice-cream which may they eat, not unaccompanied with fragile biscuits.

EL eats an Airy Green Gooseberry

I know all about Tunbridge Wells. There is a bridge, & some wells, – & a Tun & then all three are smashed up together & taken in small quantities at early dawn or after sunset.

I have no more energy than a shrimp who has swallowed a Norfolk Dumpling.

. . . gooseberries may atone for much evil.

Acknowledgements

*For permission to reproduce material
in this book we are grateful to :*
Dr. B. W. Paine
The Humanities Research Center, The University of
Texas at Austin
The Somerset Record Office
The Houghton Library, Harvard University
The Pierpont Morgan Library, New York
The Tennyson Research Centre, Lincoln, by courtesy of
Lord Tennyson and the Lincolnshire Library Service
The Robert H. Taylor Collection, Princeton University
Somerville College, Oxford
K. J. Hewett, Esq.
and to the Oxford University Press for whom
Vivien Noakes and Charles Lewsen are preparing
the definitive edition of Edward Lear's nonsense.

O criky cauliflowers & little petrified periwinkles!
O barley sugar=tongs, & evangelical eyeglasses!
What more can I say ?'